WELL-OILED MACHINE

A SHORT STORY

WELL-OILED MACHINE

A SHORT STORY

JEFFERY WEAVER

Well-Oiled Machine: A Short Story

For information about this title, contact the publisher:

Pen2PadStories
jsweaver2011@gmail.com

ISBNs:
979-8-9912131-0-3 (softcover)
979-8-9912131-1-0 (eBook)

Printed in the United States of America

Cover and Interior design: 1106 Design

First and foremost, I'd like to thank my wife, who's been my number-one support system. You've always believed in me and told me to keep going. You've been there since the start of my writing journey, and I cherish story time with you. I also want to say thank you to a few others who have been involved; you have inspired and motivated me to keep going in my writing career.

CJ, my go-to banter buddy. From spewing ideas to providing five-dollar Friday words, our creative sessions together are always a blast. I look forward to our future sessions with the other stories that I have lined up! Perry, as one of my best friends, you have provided feedback to me not just as a peer, but as a fellow writer. It's amazing that we get to share each other's stories back and forth in their raw form, and I will forever cherish that. I can't wait to share more stories down the road! Seth, a friend who is a fan of many genres—I'm very appreciative to get the perspective from a reader's standpoint. Your feedback, from catching plot holes and continuity errors, to overall genre knowledge, has helped my story become a smooth and enticing sci-fi mystery. To Jeremie, you were there when I was still writing my stories in paper journals. What was I thinking? LOL! I would always run my ideas and stories by you. At the time, I had no writing background or knowledge, but you always made me feel like anything is possible if I just try. I tried. I wrote. Now I am published! Thanks, Jeremie, for inspiring me to pursue my dreams.

Thank you from the bottom of my heart to my beta readers. You all have been the key players in helping me hone my skills, build my vocabulary and execute my craft. Deryn, Kathleen, and Claude, thank you for your knowledge, experience, and feedback. It has played a vital role in getting this story from good to great! I've learned so much from you all, and it has helped me tremendously. My biggest takeaway from you guys is . . . show, don't tell.

Last but certainly not least, my future readers. My love for creating isn't just for me. It's for you, too. When I began writing, it started as a hobby, but I soon realized I loved it. I craved it. I thank you for taking the time to read my book. I hope you enjoy my stories, characters, and plot twists as much as I enjoyed writing them.

Contents

Chapter 1

A Glimpse into the Future

M*y eyes opened; I was lying* on a cold slab table, naked and confused.

"Welcome back from the land of the dead!" a mysterious voice said over a scratchy PA speaker.

My name is Darius Clayton, a detective from the Golden State, and I had been killed by a fucking synthetic. You might be wondering how I got here. Let me take you back to how it all started.

I've lived in California for as long as I can remember. My eagerness for justice and locking up scumbags has been there ever since I was a kid. The death of my younger brother helped solidify that. Wrong place, wrong time . . . I was told.

We were just kids, innocent kids playing outside, when the bullets started to fly. You tell me how that's fair. It was just another gang rival trying to claim turf. I was the lucky one— if you can call it that. At the end of it all, I still had a dead brother. Anarchy and lawlessness are what a world comes to when no one gives a shit. Lost loved ones and a lifetime of heartache is the end result.

My law-enforcement career started in Los Angeles. I can't remember how long I've been a detective, but it's long enough to where my boss won't quit nagging me to move up to management. Of course, I would turn that down. I told my boss, "That's where souls go to die." He always got a good chuckle out of that.

My city, LA, once thrived. The City of Angels was a place folks aspired to live. However, the future has not been kind to her. The locals here now refer to LA as "The Armpit." The whole place stinks of crypto thugs and tech punks. They run around my beloved city like they're in charge. LA is a shithole now, but it's still my home.

Cyber and neuro tech had come a long way. Some of it good. Some of it bad, but like a dog with a tick on its ass—the inevitable itch was coming. We didn't get a say in the matter nor a choice. We were just expected to accept how involved tech was in our lives and that was the end of it. Now the world was full of androids—or, as the conformed humans referred to them, "synthetic humans." Everyone was so God-damned sensitive that somehow the term "android" was offensive, like we were going to offend a piece of metal. Just because they can mimic human activity doesn't make them one of us. The worst part is that androids were programmed to be obedient like a human, but to follow orders like a soldier. The perfect duo. Yeah, fucking right. There's no such thing as perfect; never was. Eventually, everything went to hell. Androids are nothing but fake flesh and programs.

The whole reason androids had been created in the first place was to counteract against "The Chosen." No one knew much about them or how long they'd been around, but there was that incident in Maine back in the 1950s. Of course, the government tried to cover that up, but eventually the truth got out. It always does in the end.

To make matters worse, the government made it nearly impossible for The Chosen to live a normal life. Any of them caught using their powers were killed onsite. On the other hand, *I* never had a problem with them. Some of The Chosen used their abilities for good. However, there were those who wanted to see the world burn, and the government wasn't going to take any chances. The Chosen were quickly considered outlaws, and insidious new laws were put in place.

As for humans, anyone found helping a Chosen would be considered a terrorist and arrested. That was just the beginning. Humans had a chip planted in the left forearm. Some rich and power-hungry jerk in France came up with that. It was known as CodeX. The purpose of the chip was to signal anytime The Chosen used their abilities. Using their powers was against the law. According to the government, it was the only way to keep The Chosen under control. We were required to have our chip scanned when we attended any events or social gatherings. This was the government's way of enforcing crowd control. They had checkpoints set up all over, but there were those on the law-enforcement side who believed in The Chosen and helped them bypass said checkpoints . . . for the right price.

Humans—or, should I say, *politicians*—hated The Chosen more than anyone. They saw them only as a problem to society. They feared what they couldn't control . . . always have. Fear and panic drive the motivation to exterminate said problem . . . permanently. Although attempts were made for a peaceful agreement, resolution was never found. In my opinion, technology was the real monster. Some say that our tech will eventually be the *homo sapiens* killer and that soon we will be outnumbered by androids.

Doctors and scientists are the ones to blame for this mess we're in. They founded the android program. It wasn't long before the government got their greasy hands on it. Everyone has a price they're willing to sell at, and it seemed that the rights were sold to the military almost overnight. We were told that this program was going to help protect mankind, that androids were going to make humans feel safe again from The Chosen. Needless to say, that president won his third term.

Mindless pieces of metal with fake skin and fake blood. I wanted nothing more than to wipe their fake asses off the planet. I kept telling Sarge that androids are bad news, but he didn't listen. He was also blinded by their convenience. "Johnny5, get me this. Johnny5, do that." Why work harder when you can just have an android do it for you?

I tried over and over again to find flaws in the android program, but it always ended the same, and I got nowhere. My guess was that the program was sealed tighter than a gnat's ass. In the beginning, I was patient, but, over time, I grew tired and bitter. As the years passed, it was clear that I was in the minority. Humans cherished the bots more than their own family members, it seemed.

■　■　■

Chapter 2

Case 316

O*ne day, out of the blue,* Greg McClarksen, my boss, tossed me a holographic data chip, better known as an HDC. I didn't ask for the case, but he told me, with a scandalous look on his face, that I was going to want to take it.

"Come on, Darius . . . this will be right up your alley!" he said, knowing it wouldn't be.

My days of being an ambitious detective were far behind me. McClarksen continued on with his wannabe excitement. I didn't want anything to do with that case. I barely had time for the ones I was already working. I vaguely heard what McClarksen was talking about. Something to do with broken androids at the LA docks. He said "funky shit" had happened with one of the android shipments. Before he left, he told me that I was the detective for that case. He then reminded me of the Skid Row bloodbath—eighty-six murderers I had locked away.

"The data on that chip will brief you on everything you need to know," he said before closing my door.

The next morning came, and, of course, I didn't bother reviewing the HDC. Why would I? I had bigger problems to deal with. The streets were crawling with murderers and thieves. Who cared about some broken androids? It was one more nuisance I had to worry about. My thirst for vengeance for my brother kept me going, but even I had to admit I was getting tired and slow in my old age. My brain and body weren't agreeing with each other anymore. Still, a part of me thought I had what it took to burn both ends of the candle. Suddenly, my phone rang. It was McClarksen.

"HIS, link the call," I told my Home Integration System.

The AI read aloud McClarksen's contact name that I had listed him under.

"Linking call to Sergeant Dipshit, sir," HIS said in a female voice, more human-like than robot.

My boss's voice came over the speakers in my walls. Right away, I could tell he was eager by the sound of his voice. I knew why he was calling.

"Clayton, have you been briefed on the case yet?" he asked, already knowing my answer.

I fumbled my words trying to find an excuse, but before I got the chance to come up with a snide remark, he beat me to the punch.

"You have 24 hours to get yourself briefed on that case. No excuses, Clayton. Get it done!"

McClarksen's voice was stern. I guessed I was out of options at that point if I wanted to keep my job. Unwillingly, I plugged the HDC into my AI system. I was old-fashioned and hated how much technology had taken over our world, but even I had to admit that not all of it was bad. Instantaneously, the HDC brought up a tab bar that read, "Case file 316."

"HIS, open case 316," I said.

"Analyzing data . . ." HIS replied in a supple feminine voice. "Results on case file 316 found. There is also surveillance footage on case 316. Do you wish to view it, sir?"

I told HIS to show it, and, as I watched, it became evident that the footage was a less-than-ideal recording.

"HIS, pause recording there, and provide an XY axis grid display," I told it.

HIS displayed the grid layout. The camera recording was too far away and at a horrible angle. For whatever reason, there was no other footage angles from the other security cameras. That seemed coincidental. The only thing that I saw from the footage was a shipment container being opened by some dockworkers. Quickly after that, gunshots were heard. One of the shipment-container doors obscured the view of the camera. Just my luck. It's never easy. The footage never revealed what was in the container. I wasn't able to see anything substantial, and, even worse, I had no proof that androids had killed those men down at the docks.

"Holy shit!" I whispered, with my eyes wide in disbelief. "McClarksen was right. Some funky shit is going on. HIS, voice-over the case file . . ."

"Right away, sir . . ." HIS replied while opening the file. "A new shipment of synthetic humans is showing to be defective and breaking their protocol of human endangerment. They are speculated to have murdered workers down at the LA shipping docks. Families of workers will not be told about the deaths of their loved ones until defective synthetic humans are brought in and diagnosed for flawed data programming. As it stands, synthetic humans are to be considered classified as weapons of mass destruction and extremely hostile. This compudoc is to remain alpha classified. Families of the deceased will be notified after the diagnosing. End of file 316," HIS informed me.

■　■　■

Chapter 3

Partners

T*he next day, I met up* with McClarksen at his office. We went over the case together. He saw the anticipation in my eyes, and why shouldn't he? That case was my chance to prove my point and shut the android program down. A part of me was confused, though. McClarksen was an android user himself. He knew that I'd been able to solve every case I'd been involved with. What would he do if the androids were recalled? Shit . . . what would the world do if there were no more androids? Probably shut down.

"I gotta ask, Sarge. Why me? You know my hatred for the bots," I told him.

His reply was simple.

"Because . . . you're the best at what you do, Darius. You deliver. Yeah, it might not be with a pretty bow on top, but you get the job done, and if this is true about androids killing humans, then I stand on the side with my best Detective."

Suddenly, there was a knock on his door.

"Right on time. Come in!" McClarksen said from behind his large oak desk and tall leather-bound chair.

In walked a middle-aged man with peppered hair. He walked with an almost unnoticeable limp to the untrained eye, but I spotted it. Behind him was a brute of a man who almost had to wedge himself through the door to fit. His shoulders were broad, his head was shaved, and the right side of his face was disfigured, perhaps from shrapnel. His right eye was dead, with a milky discoloration.

"Detective Clayton, I presume?" the man with a limp said as he reached out to shake my hand.

I nodded my head, slowly and confused, unsure what was going on. He introduced himself; it was a name I would never forget.

"I'm Sheriff Kane, but you can call me Oryan since we'll be working together on this case," he said confidently.

"McClarksen, what the hell is this? You know I work alone."

McClarksen tried his best to defuse the situation. He told me that Sheriff Kane and him went way back to the academy days and were like brothers. He said it as if it was supposed to make me feel better.

"This is Detective Vernon," McClarksen said, pointing to the ogre in the room. "He'll be your point of contact for this case. Any clues, leads, or witnesses, you keep Vernon in the loop."

"I. said. I. work. alone," I repeated unenthusiastically.

McClarksen got rattled up at my response.

"Damnit, Clayton! I'm not sending my best on this case without some backup. It's too dangerous, even for you. Vernon is your point of contact—let that be the end of it. Understood?"

"Sure thing . . . boss," I said condescendingly as I left his office.

I grabbed my trench coat off his coat rack and made my way toward the exit of the building. As I walked away, I overheard McClarksen talking to Kane and Vernon. He told them that they just needed to give me time, that I would eventually come around. Unfortunately, time wasn't going to fix anything. I worked alone. It was better that way. I was told not to feel responsible for my brother's death, but I did anyway. It was supposed to have been a quick grocery run for my mom. On the way home, we stopped and played. It was my idea. We should've never stopped. Doesn't matter now—he's dead, and I don't work with partners.

On the sidewalk, I pinged my location for a hovercab to give me a ride over to the shipping docks. My vehicle was still in the shop. It had a blown hover thruster. I guess that's what I got for trying to replace it myself. It was a bit of a drive to the docks, especially given the time of day. Since I had the time, I rewatched the footage on the HDC, trying to see if I might have missed anything. It was time for me to pay a visit to the crime scene. I knew McClarksen wanted me to keep Vernon in the loop, but I was doing this alone.

■   ■   ■

Chapter 4

The Docks

An *hour-and-a-half* and bumper-to-bumper traffic later, I arrived. The highway was full of shitheads, cutting people off in their hovercars and glidecycles. I exited the cab and took a long breath in. The air had a thin layer of smog to it, almost like a haze. It was nothing new, though. When I looked at the port, I had to stop and admire the view. It had been years since I'd been to the docks. I watched the waves as they crashed into the port. Something about it was . . . peaceful. Kind of ironic, though, since I was there to solve a murder case. The man in the cab honked his horn and held up his left forearm, where his chip was, indicating to pay him. My cold stare let him know I understood as I placed my forearm on the cab door, where the chip reader was, and slid it forward. A small vibration in my arm let me know when it was paid.

"Damnit! Is there anything that doesn't cost an arm and a leg anymore?" I said once I saw the cost.

The hovercab sped off and left a cloud of smog behind. I was left at the docks to do what I do best. At first, I thought I was at the wrong place. There was no crime-scene tape. No evidence markers. Nothing. It was odd. From all my years of detective work, this signaled to me an obvious cover-up. A lot of detectives would be confused, but ones with experience know better. Androids were programmed to fix any messes they'd caused, including hiding bodies now, I guessed. I needed to be patient. Still, something about it didn't sit right in my gut. Call it intuition or experience—either way, something was off.

Given the gravity of the situation, I needed to work fast and find anything that was going to give me a leg up on the case. The odds of solving a case drops by half after the first forty-eight hours. That was twenty-four hours ago. Evidence can be preserved for only so long before it's damaged or even destroyed, even in our high-tech days. McClarksen wanted me on that case because I was the best. Two hundred and ninety-nine cases solved, and I never had a case go cold. That meant I was on a serious time crunch.

I wouldn't be the only one looking for those murder bots. The government would be looking for their precious property, trying to sweep away their fuck-up like nothing had happened. They couldn't afford to jeopardize the trust they'd built with humans, even if that meant a few people died along the way. If the androids were truly defective, the government would ensure that the military do everything to prevent that secret from getting out to the public. The world would be in shambles if humans found out that androids weren't killing only The Chosen anymore. It was my job to expose that. As I progressed further into the port, I was met by a man who walked out of his trailer office. He was wearing a hat pulled down slightly—just enough so I couldn't get a full make of his face.

"Can I help you?" the man said.

"You in charge here?" I said, with my back facing him.

I didn't give the man the courtesy to face him when talking. My attention was elsewhere, looking at the surroundings, observing, seeing if I could determine anything that wasn't in the HDC surveillance footage. At a quick glance, everything seemed normal. I continued to walk around to get a closer look at the other containers. I looked for any damage or signs of struggle, blood spatter, or casing shells. The man with the hat followed me around. I knew he was trying to figure out what I was doing. I bent down next to where container 316 was in the footage. It was gone now.

"I hate to ask, but can I see some ID?" the man said.

Again, I didn't even bother turning around. Instead, I pulled my badge out, and a holo-projection with my Detective

ID number popped up. As I continued my search, he became more nervous. I could hear it in his voice.

"You mind telling me what this is all about?" he said.

I didn't answer him right away. The dirt area in front of where container 316 once was looked to have been smoothed over, like someone or something was trying to cover up tracks. It was barely noticeable, but it was just enough. I'd seen this before in my line of work. Also, the other cameras around the dock had been disabled. None of them had the small, flashing and blinking red light indicating that they were recording. The only functioning one was from the HDC. It was like it had been done on purpose . . . like it was planned. I quickly and discreetly took a photo of the security camera with my phone, hoping it could come in handy later.

The man approached. I turned around, finally catching a better view under his hat. He had a scar that went diagonally across his face from his right eyebrow down to his chin. The uncertainty in his eyes told me he knew something, but he was smart, trying to play innocent, so I played along.

"Maybe if you tell me what's going on, I could of be some help?" he said as if he cared.

"Actually, I think I have the wrong place. Sorry to have wasted your time," I told him.

I still needed a search warrant, but I had everything I needed. The place had been picked clean. Whoever had covered this up knew what they were doing and possibly had help. There was no way a single person could do all that. No evidence. No footage. No witnesses. This whole place stunk of foul play, and I knew cases weren't solved on hopes and dreams.

I shook his hand and apologized again for wasting his time. The look on his face was all I needed to confirm that he knew something, but I wasn't going to push the matter any further. I wanted to do my own homework and see what I could dig up before making any accusations. I handed him my card and told him to call if he saw anything suspicious. The man with the scar across his face held up my card in compliance and nodded his head. He watched as I started to make my way to the exit.

"Oh, by the way, where's container 316?" I said in a fake curious tone as I turned back around.

"What do you mean?" he asked, dumbfounded.

"Well, you have container 315 and 317, but where's 316?" I asked again.

The man adjusted the bill of his hat up and down. The look on his face was . . . subtle, but, like a good poker player, he kept his composure.

"It hasn't come in yet," he said confidently.

"I see. It's kind of funny that containers are being shipped out of order these days," I told him as I turned back around and left.

■ ■ ■

Chapter 5

Old Friends

I *waited out at the street* for one of those damn yellow hovercabs to take me back to my place. The sun was setting, and nightfall was upon my city. The neon billboards were slowly becoming brighter and brighter with each passing minute of the fading sun. LA lit up like a damn Christmas tree for miles. As I waited, I was met with a familiar figure lurking in the shadows. At first, I thought it was just another street punk looking to get his revenge on me for locking him up, but I was quickly corrected when he said my name.

"I thought I'd find you here, Clayton," the shadow-cast man said.

I didn't say anything—not right away, at least. By the tone of his voice, I could tell he was annoyed. With both fists clenched, I got myself ready for a fight. Out from the shadows, the man stepped into the light.

"Vernon . . . ," I said, annoyed.

"You know ya ain't supposed to be here without me. You heard what Sheriff Kane told ya," Vernon said in his cocky tone.

"I heard what he said, but that doesn't mean I give a rat's ass. As far as I'm concerned, this is my case," I said back.

Vernon came closer, towering over me by a good half-foot. He looked like something out of a monster story. It was like I could see a green stench coming from his mouth, like a dragon who has just devoured his enemy. He was mere inches from my face as we stood there in silence. He thought he could intimidate me with his stature. I didn't crack easy. Vernon could tell from my eyes that I wasn't going to back down, even though his legs were the size of my waist. His finger jabbed me in the upper left shoulder region, and he stared me in the face with his one good eye.

"Glad we have an understanding . . . 'cause I ain't here to babysit yer ass. Now . . . get in the damn car," he said, nodding his head over his right shoulder.

I didn't argue. It didn't make sense to try to wrestle a bear. Vernon opened the back door, and, immediately, I saw Sheriff Kane sitting back there. He was waiting and smoking a cigarette.

"Give ya a lift home?" he said.

I knew I was going to get an earful, but that was part of the job—or at least the way I did it. This case belonged to the

LAPD, not some Podunk sheriff's department. I got into the back seat as Vernon started the car and headed for my place. The first minute of the drive was silent. The only sound was the crackling of Kane's cigarette as he took each puff.

"I thought those things were illegal nowadays" I said, finally breaking the awkward silence.

He was mid-puff when he gave me a long, drawn-out stare before he barked out a laugh. Kane took another drag on his cancer stick as he gently clapped Vernon on the shoulder, like he was getting a good kick out of it. The big guy and I didn't join him in his laughter.

"Yeah—if you're a normal civilian, they are. Why are you over here breaking my balls, Darius? We're on the same side," Kane said.

I stole a glance at the rearview mirror, only to find out Vernon was staring at me like a guard dog, anticipating me doing something. Kane took one last drag before rolling down his window and flicking the butt outside. He blew smoke in my face and then apologized condescendingly.

"Let's cut to the chase. We have a fucked-up situation here. Androids breaking protocol isn't gonna fly. Darius, you're here because McClarksen said you're the best. Well, ol' Vernon boy here is the best, too. You can say he's somewhat like you. Not afraid to get his hands dirty—if you know what I mean. If this is true about androids killing humans, this case is gonna make history."

"What are you getting at, Kane—"

"It's Sheriff Kane, asshole! Have some respect for the ranks," Vernon interrupted.

"It's fine, Vernon," Kane assured him. "Just know that Vernon will do what it takes to get the job done. It's for your own good not to get in his way."

They dropped me off at my place, and I couldn't wait to get some fresh air. Once I stepped outside of the car, I was surprised that there wasn't much difference. Maybe it was in my head, or maybe I had became accustomed to the cigarette smell that lingered in my nose. The car's tires squealed as it sped off, leaving a small trace of grayish white smoke.

■　■　■

Chapter 6

Puzzle Pieces

I *headed inside, tossed my trench coat* on the coat hanger, and made my way straight to the kitchen. Over on the kitchen counter were two open, enclaved slots in the wall—one for coffee and the other for tea. It was time to relax and sort things out in my head. The only thing I wanted was my tea. Something about it helped me think. Now that Kane and Vernon weren't a tick on my ass, I was on my own for the case, which I preferred. Of course, I wasn't going to tell McClarksen the true intention of his so-called "brother" over at the Sheriff's Department. It was probably for the best. McClarksen was a stand-up guy. It would definitely crush him knowing that his friend was just like everybody else—willing to sell out to make the quick dollar and become famous.

"HIS, make my evening cup of tea."

"Right away, sir. Shall I make your favorite, Earl Grey, or would you like to try something new?"

"Keep it basic. Keep it simple. That's the problem nowadays. Everyone thinks they got the next best idea that's going to change the world," I said, disgruntled.

HIS began to make the tea. As I waited, I sat at my kitchen table. It was time to start putting the pieces of the puzzle together. I knew the man at the docks was a lost cause for any anonymous tips. However, something in my gut told me he was connected to the missing container 316. I just needed to figure out the how and why.

How does a whole container of defective androids go missing? Somebody knew something. The evidence was out there, and I needed to find it first, now that it was a race between Vernon and me. My LAPD ID badge flipped open on the table, displaying holo-images above. It read "Username" and "Password." The badge allowed me access to city information. The holo-tech in the badges became standard issue for all law-enforcement right around the same time the android program launched. Finally, the government had gotten something right with their tech. It was a good way to keep tabs on their robotic sheep. As I logged in, that's when I remembered the cameras at the dock. I needed to find out if there was any other footage before the other cameras got disabled.

Just two minutes later, HIS informed me that the tea was done. A perfect amount of time to let the tea steep. I walked over and grabbed the piping hot mug with the white steam coming from the top. I placed it next to me on the table, letting it cool. I continued to work. Minutes turned to hours. Before I knew it, I was in deep. I was like a madman on a mission, treating it like it was my last.

I looked up everything accessible to me—everything from different security-camera companies, makes, and models, and employees working at the dock that day to truck delivery companies. For the trucking companies, I used Black Box Data. This held navigational data and direction of travel. This was useful for narrowing down which trucks delivered to the dock. I was able to find out the common route the trucks took and who was working the day the container went missing.

Before I knew it, I had worked through the night, ultimately forgetting about my tea. Pulling an all-nighter wasn't uncommon in my line of work. All the information was there now. I had names, companies, and timestamps. Now it was time for some old-fashioned interrogation work—my favorite!

The sun was starting to come up, and that's when I decided to call it, but then my phone rang. I looked over to HIS to check the caller ID, but it read "Unknown." Maybe the guy at the dock had had a change of heart and was giving me a call to help make my job easier. That was wishful thinking. I knew it wasn't him, and, against my better judgment, I answered.

"This is Detective Clayton," I said, in a monotone.

I waited for a few seconds, but there was no response, only what sounded like static and breathing. I answered again, only this time a bit more aggressively.

"Who the hell is this?"

Again, no one answered, and the call ended abruptly. It had lasted only fifty-eight seconds, just shy of a minute so I couldn't trace the call. Either it was a prank, or someone knew what they were doing. Either way, it got my attention. The chances of it being a prank were slim to none. Especially calling *me*—of all people—the day after the container with defective androids had gone missing. It was all too coincidental, and I don't believe in coincidence.

■ ■ ■

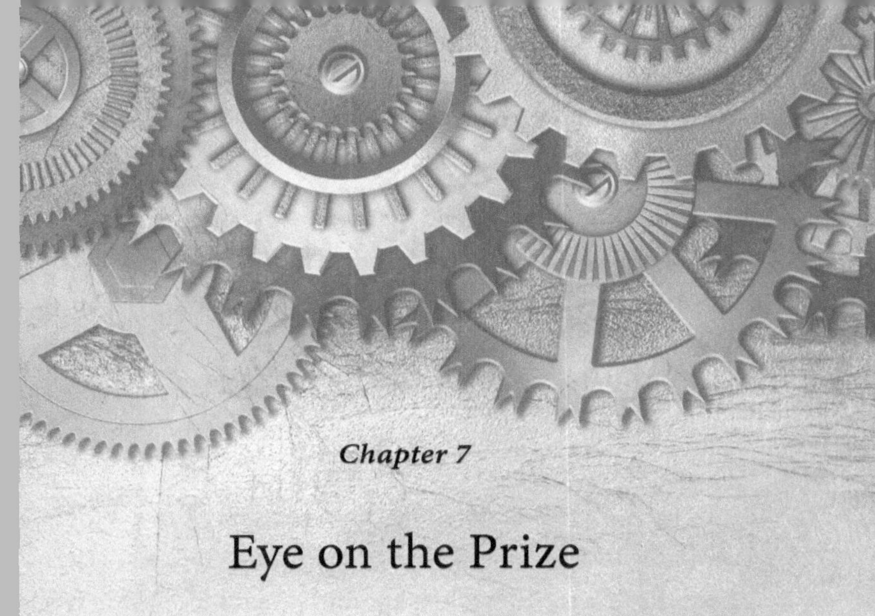

Chapter 7

Eye on the Prize

G*rabbing my trench coat off the rack*, I took what information I had gathered and headed out the door. Before I started my day, I stopped at a local diner called Gabby's. It was just a small, family-owned place. Not a lot of those places left nowadays—where actual humans take your order. Its interior displayed its original theme from the '50s, with its black-and-white checkered flooring. There was a jukebox near the entrance, and the tabletops and barstools were blue, cheap plastic leather. I sat in the far back-left corner. That's where my late wife and I had always sat. Call it tradition. Call it not letting go. Call it whatever.

After breakfast, I made a phone call to McClarksen to let him in on what I knew so far. I told him about the cameras, the trucking companies, and the employees working that day and potential ex-employees who could have a possible motive.

"Nice work, Darius. Be sure to get Sergeant Kane and Vernon up to speed."

I told him what he wanted to hear, but I had no intentions of handing over my hard work over to Dipshit One and Dipshit Two.

"Listen, Darius . . . this case is top-secret sensitive. We're dealing with what could change the future. We're talking about the deactivation of the android program."

"You're talking like you don't want me to solve this thing," I told him.

"Not at all. Just keep your head on a swivel is all I'm saying. Androids aren't defective unless they are programmed that way. So, whatever happened at the docks must have come from the top, but before we can get there, we need proof."

I reassured him and hung up the phone. If McClarksen thought the government was behind this, then we were in a bigger shitstorm than I thought. I didn't have a second to lose.

■　■　■

Chapter 8

Purposely Suspicious

M*y first stop was to some electronic stores.* I got to asking questions of some tech guys who knew about security cameras. I showed them the picture I'd taken of the security camera from the docks. They informed me that that specific camera was no longer being made and had been discontinued years ago.

"Those cameras had faulty wiring that would cause them to overheat. A lot of them would spontaneously combust into flames and were considered a safety hazard. Every business was forced to switch to these cameras"; he pointed over to the newest version of security cameras. "If not, they are breaking safety protocol . . . that or trying to fly under the radar about something."

I thanked him for his time and left. It was clear why there wasn't any other footage from the docks. Either that or some-one knew about the disabled cameras and never reported them. All I knew was that time was working against me. It had almost been forty-eight hours since the incident, and my proof of any visual evidence was looking nonexistent. A cabby drove me to the docks. I needed to be sure that there wasn't any footage from their security room.

When I arrived, it was like *all hands on deck.* The place was busy. Workers everywhere. Shipping containers were being stationed and unloaded. It was as if everything was normal. A man saw me pondering. He was the supervisor on shift that day. He asked if I needed help with something. I told him who I was and that I was investigating the missing container 316. I was quiet about the defective-androids part of the story. I had no proof yet to say otherwise. His next response fueled my frustration.

"I thought I already spoke to one of your guys this morn-ing," he said.

Immediately, I knew he was talking about Vernon. Kane was right. He was good. The worker must have seen that the expression on my face had changed because he suddenly decided to offer his help.

"I'm more than happy to go over my statement again, if that will help," the man said.

I cut to the chase, letting him know I needed shipping logs, any remaining camera footage from the last week, and to conduct interviews with some of the workers. Nothing was off the table until I established some alibies. The man was polite and agreed to helping. His cooperation and generosity was the complete opposite from the man with a scar on his face. That's when I described that person to the supervisor, but his response raised even more suspicion.

"We don't have anyone here who fits that description."

Right away, that put the man with the scar to the top of my list of POI, or persons of interest. I suspected he was hiding something. To get some answers, I needed to find him—and quickly. The supervisor warned me that gathering that amount of data would take several days to collect. As the supervisor left, something caught my eye. The security cameras all had blinking red lights. Something else was different, too. They had all been replaced; the new ones were just as the gentleman mentioned at the electronic store.

"Excuse me, sir!" I said, hurried, trying to catch up to the supervisor.

"Yes, Detective?"

"When did those cameras get installed?"

"I'm not sure what you mean. We've always had those cameras, ever since the older ones became a safety hazard years ago," he informed me.

The look on my face became angry. I confronted him and accused him of lying. Reaching into my pocket, I grabbed my phone to show him the picture from the day before that I had taken.

"What the hell? Where is it?" I said, enraged.

"Where's what?" the supervisor said, nervously.

I scrolled through my phone as if the photo were somehow going to magically appear. The photo was gone, but I knew I hadn't deleted it. It was as if it had never existed. The supervisor asked if there was anything else I needed. All I could do was sit there with a blank look on my face, lost to this mystery. He left me in my silence while I pondered my thoughts. I stared up at the security cameras. I knew what I saw. Those cameras hadn't been there before.

I called McClarksen, explaining the situation. He tried his best to calm me down. He told me that I needed to be patient, but patience had nothing to do with it. The fact remained that evidence had been tampered with. Of course, McClarksen blamed it on my lack of sleep and stress. He told me to get some rest and come at it with fresh eyes. Hell, maybe he was right, but something told me otherwise. Maybe it was because I had been waiting for a case like this ever since the android program had gone into effect. It wasn't that I hadn't had bad feelings before, but this case felt . . . different. Either that, or I was losing my edge.

■　■　■

Chapter 9

Data

Hours *turned into days.* I wasn't going to sit on my ass and do nothing while I waited for the information to be handed to me. I had HIS generate a picture of the man with the scar on his face. I made sure that those images were shown on the screens all through town, in hopes of exposing him. At the same time, I did some old-fashioned detective work by knocking on doors and finding out if anyone had seen or heard anything. Of course, everyone answered the same. Nobody saw anything.

With each passing day, I kept to my routine. I'd go to the diner. After that, I called the supervisor to see if shipping container 316 had been delivered. After being told "No," I still headed down there to check for myself. If there was anything

I'd learned in all my years in law enforcement, it was "See it with your own eyes—just to be sure." The container wasn't there, though.

While I waited for the security footage to be gathered, I conducted interviews with the workers down at the station. One by one, they all gave me their statements, sounding like a broken record. Every damn one of them checked out clean, with solid alibies, and even passed a polygraph test. I went as far as reaching out to ex-employees, especially some who, I thought, had motive, but even that failed. Those employees were either locked up, dead, or had moved away.

Just three days later, I got a phone call from the supervisor from the docks. He told me that he had the one-hundred-and-sixty-eight hours of footage for me. I didn't have him send it over to me. I went to the docks and picked it up instead. If there was a shred of evidence, I didn't want it getting hacked or altered in any way. So far, I had nothing else going for me, and that footage was either going to give me a break in the case, or it would be just another dead end.

As I left the docks with the footage, I ran into Kane and Vernon; they both began staring at me like I had something they wanted. Vernon was leaned against the side of the building, picking his teeth with a toothpick, while Kane was smoking a cigarette. Kane puffed out a cloud of smoke, and then a shit-eating grin appeared on his face.

"The man of the hour!" Kane exclaimed. "Sorry. 'Detective,' I mean."

My mouth stayed closed for once. I had no small talk with which to counter. All I wanted to do was get back to my place and have HIS analyze the footage, but Kane and his goon weren't going to let me off that easy.

"Whatcha got there, Detective?" Kane said in a cynical tone.

"It's called suck my ass . . . Sheriff," I replied back, sardonically.

Vernon flicked his toothpick to the ground and pushed off the wall. The intense look on his face meant that he wanted to peel my flesh back as if I were a banana, but Kane suddenly waved him off.

"Fortunately for you, Clayton, I respect McClarksen. I don't think he'd appreciate his best Detective's face looking like a cheese grater had gotten to it. Let him through," Kane ordered Vernon.

I walked past them both, a half-smirk on my face.

"Good dog," I told Vernon condescendingly.

■　■　■

Chapter 10

Cold Case

A*t home, I didn't waste any time.* HIS started playing the security footage from the docks. I finally felt like I was getting somewhere. Now that I had my ducks in a row, I thought it was going to be easy as one, two, three. I should had known that the case wasn't going to be wrapped up like a Christmas gift with a pretty bow on top. No, this was going to be like trying to find a pile of shit at a dump site. Before I knew it, two weeks had gone by, and I still had no breadcrumbs on shipping container 316. On top of that, there was still no hit on the man with the scar across his face. He had probably ditched town by now.

A month went by. Then two. The surveillance footage came back clean. The shipping logs were all legit, too. Things hadn't gone in my favor. I had nothing. Not one shred of evidence found. McClarksen wanted to pull me from the case, but I was determined.

The nail in the coffin came when McClarksen found out I wasn't working with Kane and Vernon. He said he was disappointed but not surprised. I took that as I was still assigned to the case. After a three-month dry spell, McClarksen told me that it was time to accept the fact that the case had gone cold.

My first ever. Shit. I couldn't admit it. There had to have been something I was missing, but the case was slowly slipping out of my grasp. Maybe it was pride. Maybe it was obsession, but I wasn't going to quit. I couldn't just walk away. I couldn't let McClarksen take me off the case. I had come too far to let the government sweep another one of their fuck-ups under the rug. I needed to look at the case from another perspective. Needing to clear my head, I went to the diner to think.

■　■　■

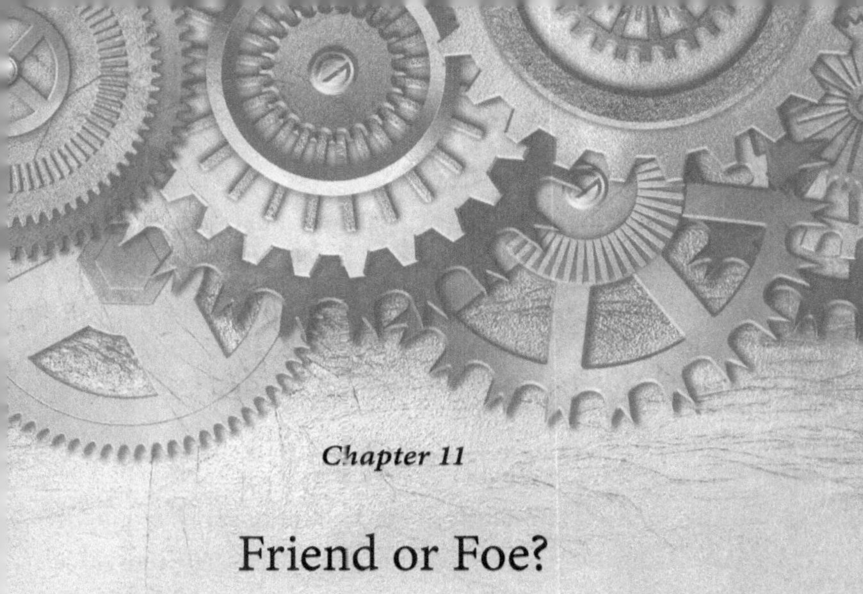

Chapter 11

Friend or Foe?

A*t the diner, I sat where I always did,* in the back far-left corner. The morning started off like any other. I ordered my usual. Two eggs over easy with three—not two, but three— thick slices of bacon and a piece of toast with a piping hot mug of coffee. The food was brought out, and, immediately, the smell was intoxicating. Just as the coffee cooled down to a drinkable temperature, that's when it happened. The door to the diner burst open; an android, who had to duck down to enter, was now in the foyer.

"My program indicates a hostile has used their powers in this establishment. Reveal yourself, Chosen!" the android said in its robotic tone.

It didn't look like your typical household-dailies android. It didn't have the fake skin but, instead, looked purposely unfinished. The exposed synthetic-fiber wires in its neck made a soft clicking sound as its head scanned the room from left to right. At that moment, I placed my hands under the table, right next to my Smith and Wesson, ready for things to go south. The android stepped forward, with its heavy-metal feet making thuds and causing subtle vibrations throughout the diner. One by one, it started to scan the scared individual diners. It was ironic that humans were supposed to feel safe around these bots, and, yet, the look on everyone's faces was the opposite.

The diner was in utter silence, and the people seemed to be trembling . . . everyone except me. My gun hand stayed calm and relaxed, off the trigger. The massive bot got closer and closer until it was within an arm's length of me. I lowered my head, looking down, but I kept the robot in the corner of my eye. That bastard stood almost eight feet tall, as opposed to the normal ones that were merely six. The other glaring difference was its eyes. They shone a dark-yellow glow. All the other androids had a blueish-purple light coming from their eyes. Something was very different about this one. Maybe it was one from the shipment container 316? The ogre of an android suddenly stopped. It looked at the man sitting at the diner bar area across from me. His back was to me and the android. Without warning, the android reached its arm toward the stranger.

"I wouldn't do that if I were you," the stranger said in his calm Eastern accent.

The emotionless piece of metal, of course, didn't listen. Quickly and quietly, I unholstered my weapon, keeping it hidden under the table. The android was about to place its hand upon the man's shoulder. Before I reacted, the man reached over his shoulder, grabbed the arm of the massive robot, and launched it over the diner bar with ease. The eight-foot bag of bolts was flung over the bar and crashed into the kitchen area. The cooks frantically got out of the way, but one of them wasn't so lucky. She was killed instantly, crushed like a can of pop by the weight of the synthetic.

Everything happened in what felt like a blink of an eye. The unknown man at the diner bar quickly stood up from his chair, walked over to the downed synthetic, and took ahold of its arm. He gave several forceful yanks and pulled the android's arm off. Sparks and oils began to spill out as the strange man turned around and finally revealed his face. His inner pupils were glowing a true blue. That's something only a Chosen could do. I noticed the massive scar that went diagonally across his face from his right eyebrow down to his chin. It was the man from the shipping docks. As much as I wanted to bring this man in for questioning, I knew getting between an android and a Chosen was not my place.

By the time I realized what was going on, the android was already back on its feet. Now its eyes glowed a distinct shade of dark yellow, almost orange, like it was switching modes. The older models did this, but with a dark cherry red. The manufacturers said it helped humans visualize synthetic emotions. The people in the diner saw that, too, and started to panic as they began to run and scream in all different directions.

Except for the man with the glowing blue eyes and me. He did try to make a break for the front entrance. He knew reinforcement androids were on the way and that he would soon be outnumbered.

The one-armed android created a focused light from its optics that instantly beamed and hit the Chosen, who was trying to escape, in the right upper back. He was knocked to the ground, writhing in pain at first. I thought he was about to be killed, but, to my surprise, he quickly shook off the pain and got back to his feet. I could see his skin was . . . moving. It was coming together, and the wound soon faded into a scar. That's when he took cover, flipping over a nearby diner table.

■　■　■

Chapter 12

The Chosen

"*B*raddik Hanver!" the android said in a loud, authoritative voice. "You are to be brought in, dead or alive, for the deaths of eighty-six synthetic humans."

"You have to have a consciousness in order to be considered dead," Braddik yelled from behind the table.

I held my revolver up, aiming it directly between the eyes of the android, ready to take the shot, but Braddik revealed himself from behind the table. A fog gently filled the ambient air around both of his arms. This wispy water vapor crackled as his arms frosted over. Suddenly, from thin air, massive, jagged, and sharp ice shards were produced, and he hurled them toward his enemy. The speed at which Braddik threw them caused a whistling sound as they zipped by. They hit the android—two in the left leg and one in the middle of its chest. That would slow it down for only a few minutes. I left my position in the back-left corner and ran toward the Chosen, Braddik. As I passed the android, I slid on the ground and kicked one of its legs out from beneath it. I popped back up to my feet, leapt over the flipped table, and lay on the checkered floor next to Braddik.

"You're a goddamn Chosen, huh! Should have known," I said, pissed.

"Good to see you again, too," he said, referring to our meeting at the docks.

"When we get out of this, your ass is coming back with me to the station," I told him.

"Don't you mean, 'if'?" he replied.

I had to do something to keep the bot from killing my only suspect in the case. I picked myself up off the floor and stood, facing the android.

"LAPD! Stop right there!" I yelled.

It was no use. The android had removed one of the shards from its leg and threw it back at us. When the ice shard impacted the table, it almost destroyed it completely. Splintered wood and ice fragments were flying everywhere. Our cover was gone. Some of the ice that hit Braddik disappeared, as if being absorbed into him. The robot removed another ice shard and threw it, but, this time, Braddik and I both rolled out of the way, taking cover behind another nearby table. I halfway expected my adrenaline to kick in or at least feel some shaking in my knees, but I was steady as ever. Peeking from behind the table, I noticed that the android was primarily focused on the Chosen. Out of an act of desperation, it seemed, Braddik looked at me like he had a plan.

"Chosen, this is your last warning. Surrender or be decapitated," the android said.

"Do you trust me?" Braddik said.

"I'm not even going to answer that."

"I have a plan that will get us outta here alive," he went ahead with explaining. "I'm going to fake surrender and then freeze it so we can make a run for it."

There was no time to talk him out of it. Braddik had already stood up and announced his fake surrender. My revolver stayed at the ready, waiting for shit to go even further south. As Braddik stood there with his hands up in the air, I could see that the android had no intentions of keeping him alive.

Without hesitation, the android powered up its optics again, and I knew I had to act fast. I stood up just as the android shot one of its beams at Braddik. At the same time, I unloaded six rounds of my revolver. I hit all my shots—where vital organs would be in a human—hoping that I might slow it down. My bullets barely made the damn thing flinch, but it did enough to distract it, so Braddik could make an escape.

The android quickly rotated its torso at me, with its yellow-orange-ish eyes, aimed its one good arm at me, and opened fire before I could even move. Out of its wrist fired what looked like the tips of arrows. They hit me in several places with fierce velocity and exited through me as if I were paper. One of them pierced the artery in my leg, and two others tagged me in the stomach. It all happened so quickly that I didn't need my adrenaline to help me from feeling any pain. The only thing that my brain registered was that I knew these wounds were fatal. I'd worked enough cases to know how this ended. It was only a matter of time. In a last-ditch effort, I attempted to reload my gun as the android began to walk toward me. It soon towered over me, and all I saw was dark orange eyes. That was it. Fate was going to have its way with me. I didn't fight it. I let whatever was about to happen, happen. As the android stared down at me, its orange glowing eyes went to yellow. That meant only one thing: It was reverting and now didn't see me as a threat or an enemy. Why did it do that? Why was the android sparing me?

"You. You would betray us?" it said.

"'Us'?" I repeated, befuddled.

Then the android's eyes went back to their dark-orange glow, and it aimed its wrist directly at my face. Death had never scared me. I embraced it. I brought my head closer to the android's weaponized wrist, awaiting my fate. Just as it was about to fire, I heard a familiar voice call out.

■　■　■

Chapter 13

Wizard
of Androids

"*Enough!*" the voice said.

Suddenly, the android disarmed itself, and its eyes changed back to yellow. It stood upright and looked as if it were awaiting orders. I was confused nonetheless.

"Model two nine nine, standby mode," the familiar voice ordered.

The android did as it had been told: it stepped off to the side of me and powered down. Its head lowered toward the floor, and the lights to its eyes would blink white on and off, signifying it was in standby mode. From out of the back of the diner, a man in a suit revealed himself. The suit was all black, with a blood-red tie. His face finally emerged from the shadows.

"McClarksen? What the fuck is going on? What is this?" I said angrily, while clinging to life.

"I'm afraid it's a bit more complicated. Model three one six. Allow me to introduce myself. My name . . . my real name is Doctor Daemon Keer," he said matter-of-factly.

"Three one six? Like the container from the docks? I don't—"

"I know this is going to be a lot to . . . take in, but, you're my latest model of the synthetic human androids," he interrupted.

"You're lying. McClarksen—this is bullshit!" I said, becoming more furious.

"This was all a part of your memory program," he continued.

"I worked a lot of cases dealing with androids. I think I would know if I were one," I told him.

"The dock case was never real. It was merely a simulation, three one six."

"Stop calling me that! I want some goddamn answers."

McClarksen paused for a moment, while a dissatisfied look spread over his face.

"As you wish, Detective. The truth is . . . you were designed to see if we could produce simulated emotions and to develop AI consciousness. This was better known as Project Limitless, and I must say, you have performed beyond our expectations!"

"'Our'?" I said, with my eyes narrowing.

"Oh, where are my manners? Mr. Hanver, you can come back in here now. He knows," McClarksen said out loud.

The Chosen, Braddik, casually came walking back into the diner, as if nothing had ever happened. I couldn't believe what they were seeing. I was still trying to make sense of it all.

"You work for him!?" I said to Braddik in a tone of disdain.

"I wouldn't exactly say 'work.' More like, we have an agreement. Hey, by the way—no hard feelings, huh?" Braddik said.

"'No hard feelings'? I put my life on the line for you—and for what? Now I'm going to die because of you!"

"Detective!" McClarksen—or whatever his name was—butted in. "Think about it! Any normal human who sustained the injuries you just did would already be dead or close to."

I finally looked down at my wounds. Not a speck of blood was coming out of me. Instead, I was leaking fluids. There was no pain because there were no organs that had been perforated. The thought of defeat and disgust grew on my face. Everything Keer was saying was true. He wasn't Sergeant McClarksen anymore. The only thing I knew was that I didn't know anything. I slowly began to stand back up; I brushed myself off from the debris. Keer could see the long gaze in my eyes that meant I was battling my inner thoughts.

"When was the last time you remember eating? Drinking?" he continued on.

I glanced back at the table in the back-left corner of the diner. The plate of food and coffee, untouched. It was all true. I couldn't ever remember eating or drinking. Hell, I couldn't even remember being tired at the end of the day. I became more frantic at that point; I wasn't doing well in accepting my reality. My breathing became heavy. I was losing it. How could I not know?

Keer took a step toward me like he wanted to comfort me like a father would his scared son. I immediately planted one foot back in a gun-ready position as I aimed my revolver at him. He stopped in his tracks and held his hands up. I didn't break eye contact as I grabbed the rest of my bullets from my trench coat. One by one, I reloaded my revolver.

"If I'm a synthetic, then I guess I wouldn't be able to kill you then, would I?" I said in a derogatory tone.

The gun aimed steady as I pulled back the hammer. I even squinted one eye to let him know that I was serious.

"You're just frightened, three one six," Keer said as he slowly lowered his hands. "The CodeX DNA from Braddik and my Neuro tech gave life to these emotions: real emotions, like humans'. Can't you see . . . you're my greatest creation yet."

As I took in what Keer was saying, this grimly casual realization fell even deeper into my brain—if I could even call it that anymore. My vision fixated on my hands, knowing that I was nothing more than metal and wire beneath my skin. I could feel Doctor Keer staring at me. He wanted me to praise him like he was some kind of god. I wasn't going to give him the satisfaction. I had other plans.

"I said . . . don't call me 'three one six.' My name . . . is Darius Clayton."

A loud bang sounded, leaving a ringing sound throughout the diner. I had pulled the trigger the second the words left my lips. Unfortunately, the bullet only grazed his arm. I went to pull the trigger again, but my finger wouldn't squeeze.

"What did you do to me?!" I said, furiously.

Keer held his hand over his injured arm, with a look on his face as if he were impressed. I continued to try to pull the trigger, but it was no use. He walked over to me, not seeing me as a threat anymore.

"Magnificent. Bravo, three one six! You've excelled in every way. Unfortunately, I do believe I still have some . . . kinks to work out before you are perfect," he said, as he looked down to his bloody arm. "As you know, androids can't kill humans, especially their maker. Not even you . . . Darius. I programmed you all that way as a safety protocol. I'm sure you can understand."

A newfound anger was erupting inside of me. I wanted nothing more than to wipe that smug look off his face. I may not have been able to pull the trigger, but that didn't mean I couldn't beat the shit out of him. I went to lunge forward, but Keer yelled the word "Stasis," which put my body into a coma-like state. I couldn't move. He ordered me to put down my weapon. Slowly, my grip loosened, and I dropped my gun against my will. In that moment, I knew I was at Keer's mercy.

"Model two nine nine, awake," he commanded the other android.

Its head raised, and its eyes lit back up immediately. Keer issued a single order. He told it to fog my memory chip. The android walked up behind me and flipped open a part of my skull. I tried to move, but I was cemented in place.

"Keer! Don't do this. Don't fog my memory!" I begged.

"Shhh. It's going to be okay, three one six. You'll still have some memories. Just the ones I want you to have," he told me.

"NOO!" I gave one last yell as the android pulled something out of the back of my head, and everything went black.

My eyes opened, and I was lying on a cold slab table, naked and confused.

"Welcome back from the land of the dead," a familiar voice said over a scratchy PA speaker.

■　■　■

About
the Author

J*eff Weaver* is a fictional writer originally from Stockton, California. He works in the medical field full-time. When he's not working or has downtime, he spends it writing. His writing journey began in 2016, when, initially, he saw it as a hobby. Jeff quickly realized it was much more than that—it was an outlet. He loved the creativity aspect of writing and living as the characters from his stories. Jeff has written in several genres; Sci-fi mystery, psychological thriller, and fantasy. When he's not writing, he spends time in coffee shops thinking up and plotting out the elements in his stories. Aside from writing, he loves traveling with his family, making wine, and playing golf. His motivation and inspiration are his wife and kids. His dream is to hand down his stories to his children.

Keep in touch with Jeff via the web, social media and Patreon:
Patreon:
patreon.com/pen2padstories.com
Instagram:
@Pen2PadStories